I'm afraid too!

Laura Hambleton

for my family,
Scott and Marie

I'm afraid too!

Milet Publishing Ltd
6 North End Parade
London W14 OSJ
England
Email orders@milet.com
Web site www.milet.com

First published by
Milet Publishing Ltd in 2001

ISBN 1 84059 317 2

Printed in Singapore by Imago

Milet

I'm afraid too!

Laura Hambleton

Here lives the wooden man,

safe in the blanket of branches and leaves,
inside his home in the pine tree,
safe from the world outside.

Suddenly . . . CHOP! CHOP! CHOP!

The branches BREAK

and the tree falls to the ground.

He falls to the ground with a . . .

THUMP!

"Oh, no!" he cries in fear.

The forest turns cold and misty.
Tired and afraid, he hides under
a blanket of fallen leaves,

and closes his eye . . .

MUNCH!

Tiny six-legged creatures chew his wood,

making holes, scratches and marks on his body.

His body **Splinters**

and **cracks** at the edges.

The sky becomes brighter,
and voices echo in the trees.

One voice grows louder, and he is
snatched from the ground.

He is outside once more, in the yard, among planks of **wood** and long, *curling* branches.

His hair has fallen out, and his arms have snapped and broken in the move.

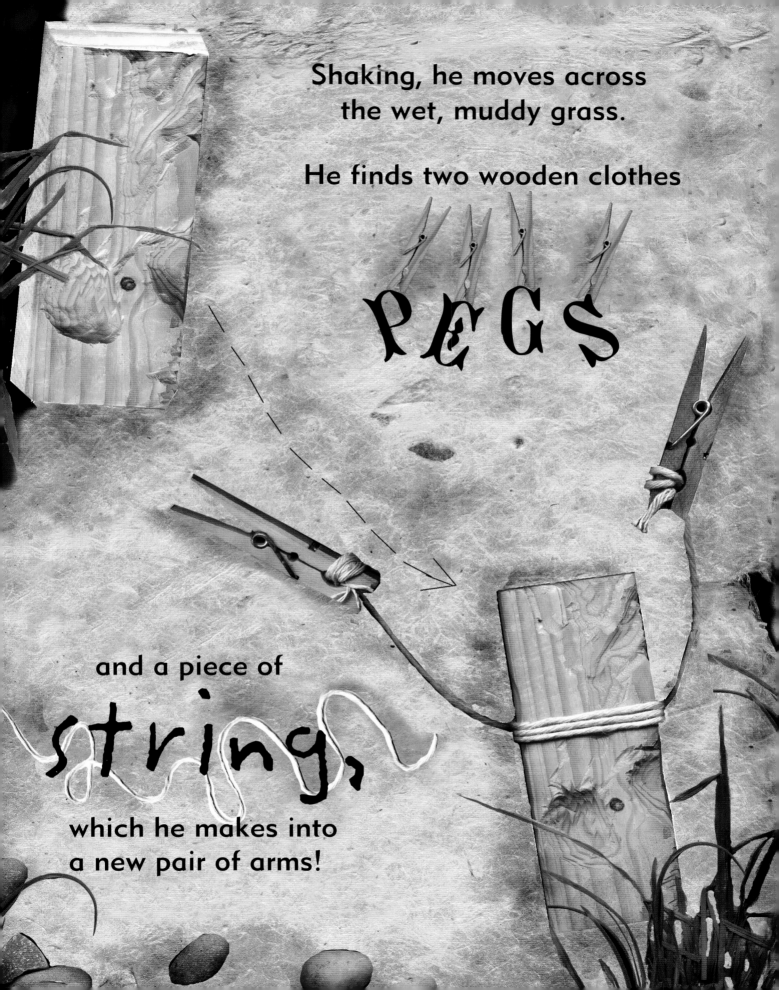

Shaking, he moves across
the wet, muddy grass.

He finds two wooden clothes

PEGS

and a piece of

string,

which he makes into
a new pair of arms!

Cold and damp,
he hangs upon
the washing line
and falls asleep . . .

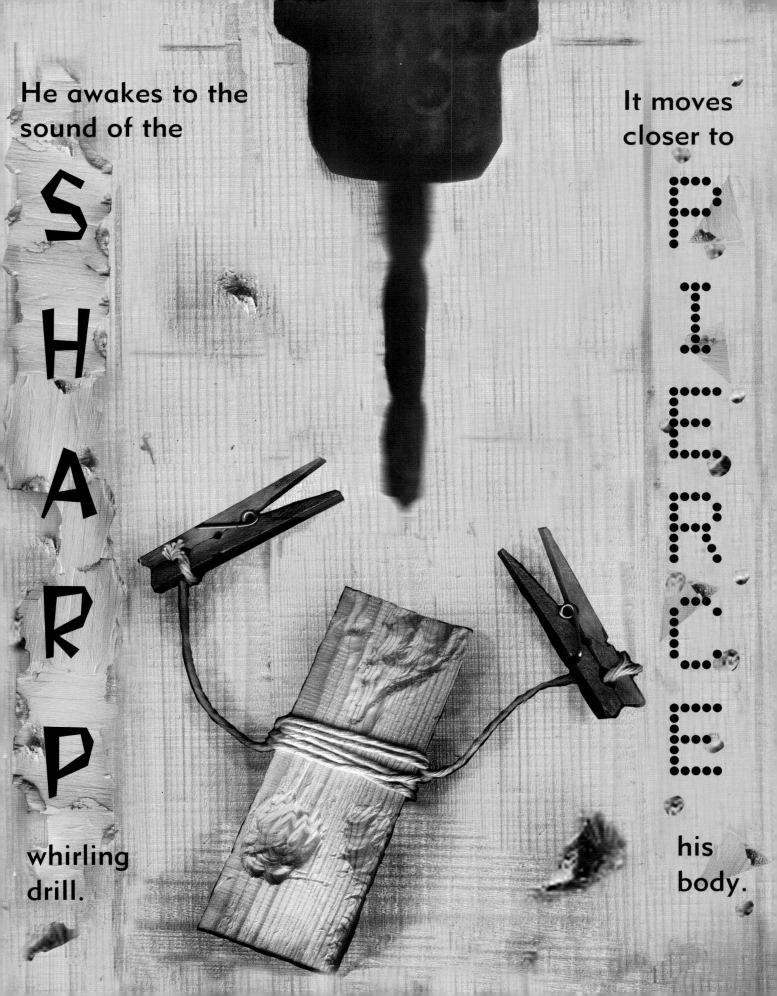

He awakes to the sound of the

SHARP

whirling drill.

It moves closer to

PIERCE

his body.

10

9

Next,

the man MEASURES him

8

with the long, thin tape measure.

7 x 3 = ?

6 - 4 = ?

5

4 + 4 = ?

3

2

What will happen to him next?

1

Scrape!  SCRAPE! Scrape!

Now he is trapped. There is no escape from the wood shaver.

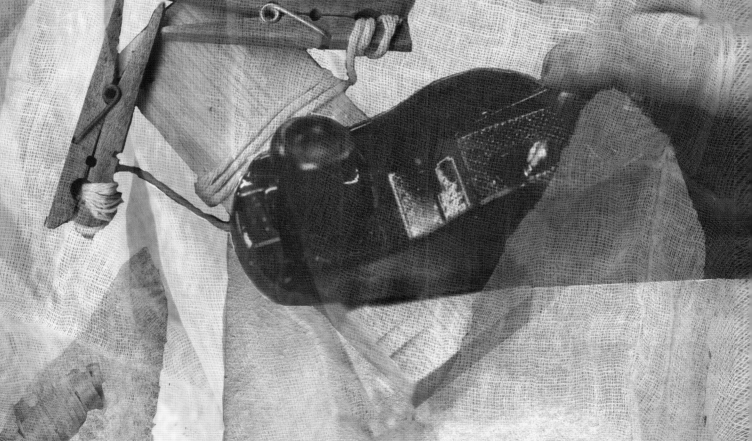

It moves left then right, tearing his surface as it moves, changing the shape of his body.

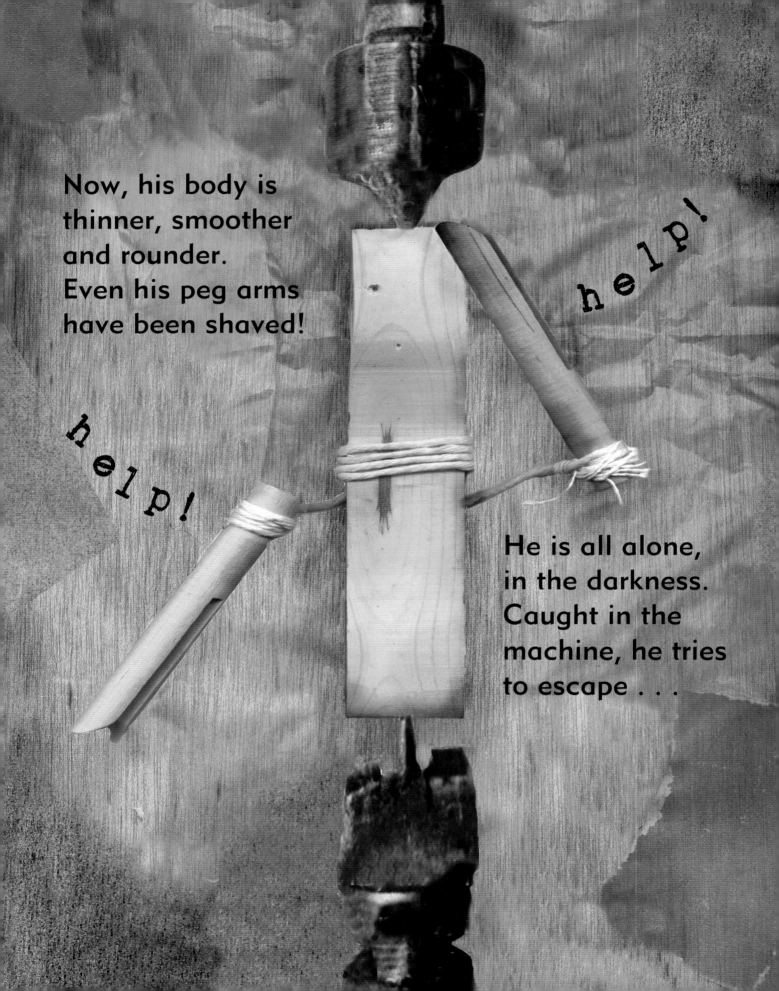

He hangs onto the side of the machine.
Then suddenly . . .

Splat!

He falls into a pot of red glossy paint.

Tired and afraid, he climbs to the top of
the paint can and clings onto a piece of wood.

He rests upon the blanket of sawdust,
and falls into a deep sleep.

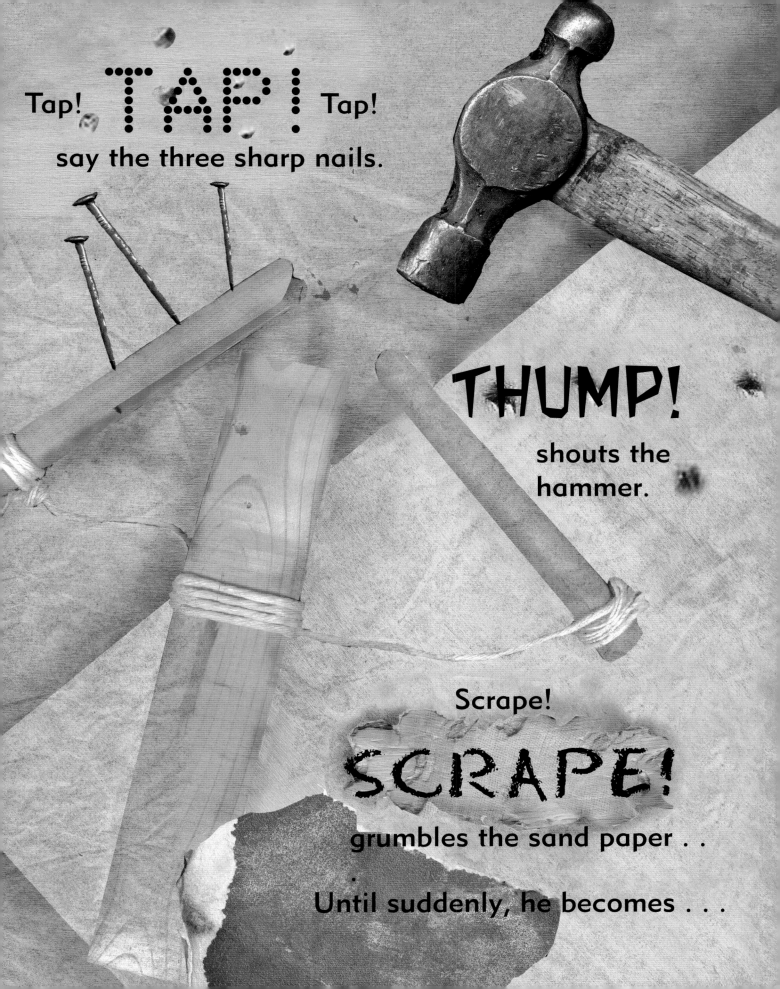

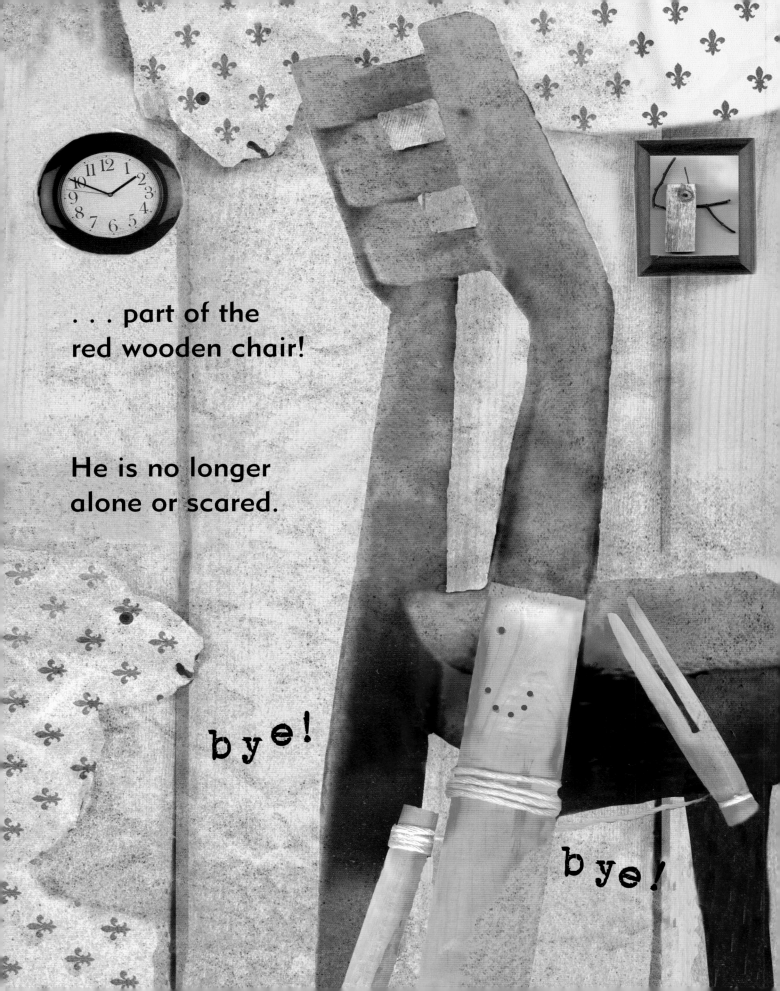

Here he stays, safe in the blanket of wood, in his home in the red pine chair, safe from the world outside.